TWO'S COMPANY

by AMANDA BENJAMIN

Viking

for
paul

My mom and I lived in a little house with willow trees growing in the garden. Every morning I'd jump into her bed and we'd sip hot tea and talk about all kinds of things. Just the two of us.

At the bottom of the garden was my secret jungle.

Lions and tigers roamed through the tall grass, and wild birds sang in the trees. Every day my mom painted in her studio and listened to music which came down into the garden. Then the tigers would swing their tails and the lions stretch their claws, and we'd dance through the grass till the sun went down.

Every night my mom and I had supper together. It was cozy and fun in our small kitchen. Sometimes we ate outside under the stars, balancing the plates on our knees.

But one night was different. Simon came for supper.

Simon had a wild black beard and he told wonderful stories. He called me Madelaine of the Willows and the Wild. After supper we stalked animals and he growled just like a tiger.

My mom liked him too. She laughed and laughed at the funny
things he said. After that evening, he often came over for supper.

Then one summer's day, my mom told me she and Simon were thinking of getting married. "What do you think, Maddy?" she asked.

"Oh, I really don't think you should," I said, diving into the water. And that was the end of that, I thought.

I still played with the lions and tigers. I still
snuggled into bed with my mom in the mornings.
But Simon was around a lot, and he
and my mom talked all the time.

Then one night my mom told me she and Simon
were going to get married. She hadn't listened
to me at all. Now Simon would always be
there with his big black beard. I wished
a wild tiger would carry him away.

Maybe my best friend could help me. Little Adam Zurka, who lived under my pillow. "Oh Adam, what should I do?" I asked him. His black button eyes stared at me for a long time. And then I heard a tiny whisper.

"Why don't you get married too?" he said. "To me."

"What?"

"Well, you love me and I love you, and if your mom's going to branch out maybe you should too."

"But Adam, you're a lizard."

"Should that stand in the way of true love?" he asked.

I thought about it. I did love Adam Zurka. He was my very best friend.

"Okay," I agreed. "Let's do it!"

I ran downstairs to my mom's studio. "I'm getting married too," I yelled.

"To Little Adam Zurka!" And I raced out of the room, leaping up the stairs two at a time.

The next morning I was woken up with a kiss. "We have a lot to do today, pumpkin," my mom told me.

"We do?"

"Oh yes, we need to buy your wedding dress and bake a cake."

"But aren't you busy today?"

"For you I have all the time in the world."

I stood up on my bed. "I want a dress the color of the sky, with sparkles on it."

My mom smiled. "Hop out of bed. We are going to find that dress at once."

I waved to Little Adam Zurka. "Good morning, good-bye," I called.
"I'm going to get my dress, and I'll probably be out all day." He gave
me a great big wink.

On the way to the store,
I asked my mom if she would
bake my cake in the shape of a tiger.
"Easy as pie," she answered as we bumped along in her car.

"Here we are," my mom said. "At the best store in town." And
it was. There were dresses everywhere. Pink ones and white
ones, spotted ones and striped ones. There were even dresses
made of silver and gold.

"Hello," my mom said to the man in the shop. "We're looking for a dress for a most special occasion. In sky blue."

"But of course, madame. I have the very thing," he replied.

The dress swirled around me like the petals of a big blue flower. "This is it!" I cried, and hugged my mom.

Afterwards we went to our favorite cafe and ordered all our favorite things. I told my mom I was going to live with Little Adam Zurka in the jungle, where I would be Madelaine of the Willows and the Wild.

"And how will you live?" she asked.

"On wild berries and coconut milk. You can come for supper
sometimes."

"We could eat under the stars," she said. "But I'd hate for you
to go away. I'd miss you so much."

Then my mom leaned over and looked into my eyes.

"Maddy, do you like Simon?" she asked me.

"Ye-es," I said slowly.

"How do you feel about him coming to live with us?"

"I don't know. Everything will change. It won't be just you and me anymore." My throat felt all choked up. "What if you start liking him more than me?"

"More than you!" she cried. "How could I? You're my own darling girl."

"But what about Simon? You love him."

"Yes, I do, Maddy, but in such a different way. Things won't be the same, I know. But nothing in the whole world could ever change how much I love you."

"Really?"

"Really and truly."

I didn't say anything for a long time. The sun shone through the leaves, making patterns on the table. Then I looked into my mom's warm brown eyes. "Do you think Simon likes having supper under the stars?"

"I don't know," she said, smiling.

"I think I'll ask him."

Illustrations done with pen and inks and watercolor.

VIKING
Published by the Penguin Group
Penguin Books USA Inc., 375 Hudson Street, New York, New York 10014, U.S.A.
Penguin Books Ltd, 27 Wrights Lane, London W8 5TZ, England
Penguin Books Australia Ltd, Ringwood, Victoria, Australia
Penguin Books Canada Ltd, 10 Alcorn Avenue, Toronto, Ontario, Canada M4V 3B2
Penguin Books (N.Z.) Ltd, 182-190 Wairau Road, Auckland 10, New Zealand

Penguin Books Ltd, Registered Offices: Harmondsworth, Middlesex, England

First published in 1995 by Viking, a division of Penguin Books USA Inc.

1 3 5 7 9 10 8 6 4 2

LIBRARY OF CONGRESS CATALOGING-IN-PUBLICATION DATA
Cohen, Amanda.
Two's company / by Amanda Cohen.   p.   cm.
Summary: Feeling threatened by the possibility of her mother's remarriage,
Maddy copes by planning her own wedding to her lizard friend Little Adam Zurka.
ISBN 0-670-84876-X
[1. Remarriage – Fiction. 2. Mothers and daughters – Fiction.] I. Title.
PZ7.C6594Tw 1995 [E]–dc20   94-39223   CIP   AC

Printed in Mexico
Set in Tiffany